CAN YOU SOLVE THE MYSTERY?

HAWKEYE COLLINS & AMY ADAMS in

THE CASE OF THE TOILET PAPER DECORATOR

& OTHER MYSTERIES

by M. MASTERS

Meadowbrook Books
18318 Minnetonka Blvd.
Deephaven, MN 55391

This book is dedicated to all the children across the country who helped us develop the *Can You Solve the Mystery?* ™ series.

Library of Congress Cataloging in Publication Data

Masters, M.
Hawkeye Collins & Amy Adams in the Case of the toilet paper decorator & other mysteries.

(Can you solve the mystery?; v. 9) Summary: Two twelve-year-old detectives solve a series of mysteries using sketches of important clues.
[1. Mystery and detective stories] I. Title. II. Title: Hawkeye Collins and Amy Adams in the Case of the toilet paper decorator and other mysteries. III. Series: Masters, M. Can you solve the mystery?; v. 9.
PZ7.M42392He   1984   [Fic]   83-23699

ISBN 0-88166-024-8 (paperback)

10   9   8   7   6   5   4   3   2   1
Printed in the United States of America.

Copyright ©1984 by Meadowbrook Creations.

Stories by Paul Bagdon.
Illustrations by Brett Gadbois.
Cover art by Robert Sauber.

CONTENTS

Would you like to become a member of the CYSTM?™ Reading Panel? See details on page 95.

Amy Adams   **Hawkeye Collins**

Young Sleuths Detect Fun in Mysteries

By Alice Cory
Staff Writer

Lakewood Hills has two new super sleuths watching over its citizens. They are Christopher "Hawkeye" Collins and Amy Amanda Adams, both 12 years old and sixth-grade students at Lakewood Hills Elementary.

Christopher Collins, the popular, blond, blue-eyed sleuth of 128 Crestview Drive, is better known by his nickname, "Hawkeye." His father, Peter Collins, who is an attorney downtown, explains, "We started calling him Hawkeye many years ago because he notices everything, even tiny details. That's what makes him so good at solving mysteries." His mother, Linda Collins, a real estate agent, agrees: "Yes, but he

Sleuths continued on page 4A

Sleuths continued from page 2A

also started to draw at a very early age. His sketches capture everything he sees. He draws clues or the scene of the crime — or anything else that will help solve a mystery."

Amy Adams, a spitfire with red hair and sparkling green eyes, lives right across the street, at 131 Crestview Drive. Known to many as the star of the track team, she is also a star math student. "She's quick of mind, quick of foot and quick of temper," says her teacher, Ted Bronson, chuckling. "And she's never intimidated." Not only do she and Hawkeye share the same birthday, but also the same love of mysteries.

"If something's wrong," says Amy, leaning on her ten-speed, "you just can't look the other way."

"Right," says Hawkeye, pulling his ever-present sketch pad and pencil from his back pocket. "And if we can't solve a case right away, I'll do a drawing of the scene of the crime. When we study my sketch, we can usually figure out what happened."

When the two detectives are not playing video games or soccer (Hawkeye is the captain of the sixth-grade team), they can often be seen biking around town, making sure justice is done. Occa-

sionally aided by Hawkeye's frisky golden retriever, Nosey, and Amy's six-year-old sister, Lucy, they've solved every case they've handled to date.

How did the two get started in the detective business?

It all started last year at Lakewood Hills Elementary's Career Days. There the two met Sergeant Treadwell, one of Lakewood Hills' best-known policemen. Of Hawkeye and Amy, Sergeant Treadwell proudly brags, "They're terrific. Right after we met, one of the teachers had a whole pile of tests stolen. I sure couldn't figure out who had done it, but Hawkeye did one of his sketches and he and Amy had the case solved in five minutes! You can't fool those two."

Sergeant Treadwell adds: "I don't know what Lakewood Hills ever did without Hawkeye and Amy. They've found a dognapped dog, located stolen video games, and cracked many other tough cases. Why, whenever I have a problem I can't solve, I know just where to go — straight to those two super sleuths!"

> **" They've found a dognapped dog, located stolen video games, and cracked many other tough cases. "**

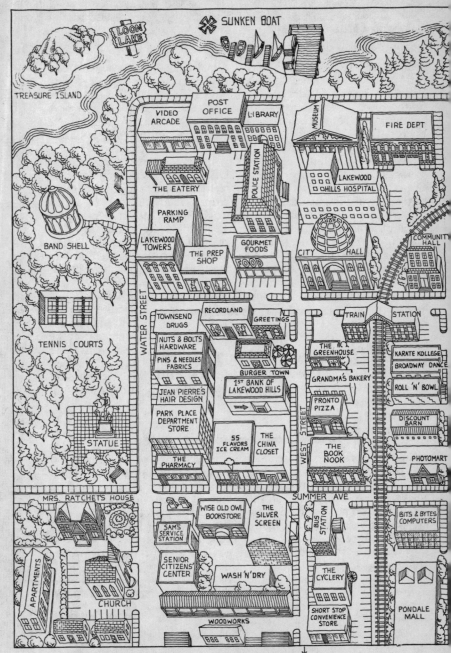

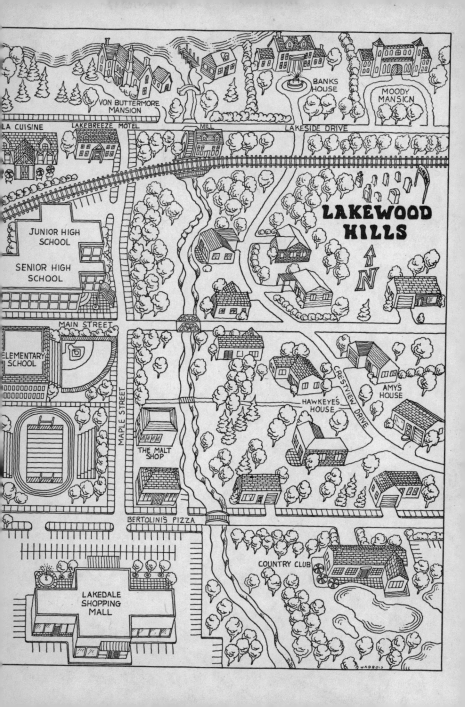

Dear Readers,

You can solve these mysteries along with us! Start by reading very carefully -- Watch out for things like what people say happened, the ways they behave, and details like the time and the weather. Then look closely at the sketch or other picture clue with the story. If you remember the facts, the picture clue should help you break the case.

If you want to check your answer-- or if a hard case stumps you -- turn to the solutions at the back of the book. They're written in mirror type. Hold them up to a mirror and they'll look right. If you don't have a mirror, turn the page and hold it up to the light. (You can teach yourself to read backwards, too. We can do it pretty well now and it comes in handy some times in our cases.)

Have fun -- we sure did!

Amy

Hawkeye

The Case of the Missing Guests

Amy Adams and Hawkeye Collins pedaled lazily along on their ten-speeds, in no particular rush to reach any special destination. The late August air was warm and clear—a perfect day. It was always a pleasure to ride on Crestview Drive, the suburban, tree-lined street where both Hawkeye and Amy lived. Their homes, in fact, were directly across from one another.

Hawkeye and Amy, both 12 and both sixth-grade students at Lakewood Hills Elementary School, were celebrities in the town of Lakewood Hills. Both were extremely interested in—and good at—solving mysteries. They'd been able to break many cases with their friend Sergeant Treadwell, of the local police department.

Two bikers approached from the opposite direction. Amy half-raised her hand in a friendly wave, then stopped in midgesture and returned her hand to the grip of her handlebars.

Neither of the two youths waved or even nodded as they passed.

"Hawkeye," Amy asked, "do you know either of those guys?"

"No . . . no, I don't. They're probably on a long bike hike. See the packs they're carrying?"

"I don't like their looks. There's something about them, Hawkeye. I'm not quite sure what it is, but there's something. . . ."

"Come on, Amy," Hawkeye said. "Sure the guys are a little scruffy, but they've been on the road for a long time.

"You're just antsy, Amy—and so am I. It's been over two weeks since Sarge has called us about any cases. To tell you the truth, I'm bored. I'd love to sink my teeth into a really big, complicated case."

Amy sighed. "Yeah, I suppose you're right, Hawkeye. I'm bored, too."

Hawkeye and Amy waved to four-year-old Curt Bingham, who lived with his family in a newly built home on Crestview Drive. Curt was playing with a bright yellow and red wagon in his driveway.

"Listen, Amy," Hawkeye said, "maybe we

could check with Sarge to see—"

A wail from in front of the Adams home cut Hawkeye short.

"AAAAAaaaaaaaammmmmmmmyyyy!!!" Lucy, Amy's six-year-old sister, ran down the driveway to the street. Tears had cut streaks down her dusty cheeks. Amy and Hawkeye stopped their bikes in front of her.

"What's the matter, honey?" Amy asked, concern obvious in her voice. "What happened?"

Lucy had to take several deep breaths before she could speak. "Kidnapping! Kidnapping!" she blurted between chokes and sobs.

Hawkeye and Amy parked their bikes. Hawkeye crouched in front of the youngster.

"Easy, now, Lucy," he said. "Catch your breath and tell us what's wrong."

"Kidnappers," Lucy began, tears flowing again.

"Wait," Amy said. "Calm down—try to relax—and tell us your problem."

Lucy made a big effort to control herself. She wiped the tears from her eyes with the backs of her hands, sniffed loudly several times, hiccupped twice, and then began to speak. Her voice cracked; she was still on the verge of tears. Amy put her hand gently on her sister's shoulder.

"Sarah and I have planned our tea party for years," Lucy said. "Last night after supper, Sarah brought all her dolls and stuffed animals over to our house—except for the woodchuck she sleeps with. They were her seven guests for our tea party. I got all my animals and dolls out, too—I have nine. We were going to have twenty-five guests for our party today."

"Sixteen," Amy said, without thinking. Lucy's lower lip began to tremble, and her eyes blurred with tears.

"*Almost* twenty-five," Amy said quickly. "Please don't get all upset again, Lucy. Go on with what you were saying. Hawkeye and I can't help you if we don't know what happened."

Lucy sniffed loudly. "OK," she said. "I pushed our picnic table—the big one—out in the middle of the grass way behind our house, where we make mud pies and build castles and roads and stuff. Then I pulled the benches over and put all our guests on them."

She paused to wipe her nose on the bottom of her T-shirt.

"I set the table with my beautiful real china tea set Gramma gave me for Christmas. I even smoothed the dirt with Daddy's rake so my footprints were almost all gone. Then I went into the house to ask Mommy to make some Kool-Aid for us, for the tea."

"Where's Sarah?" Hawkeye asked. "You two didn't have an argument, did you? Or are you trying to tell us she's been kidnapped?"

"No! We're best friends. Sarah had to go to

the dentist for a checkup before the party. She's gonna come right over when she gets back. She goes to Dr. Doan, just like we do, Amy. I didn't have any cav—"

"OK, OK," Amy said, "we get the point. Sarah's at the dentist's office. So who's been kidnapped, Lucy?"

"All the animals and dolls! Even my Kermit and my Garfield! My brand-new Garfield! And—and—"

"Take it easy, Lucy," Amy said. "We'll get your guests back. Did you see anyone around while you were setting up your stuff?"

Lucy thought for a moment. "Well, I'm pretty sure a huge flying saucer landed in the backyard and these slimy frog things with lights on their heads—"

"Lucy!" Amy cut in.

"OK. That was yesterday. But just as I was going into the house, a big bunch of cowboys on real horses rode by, looking for tea party guests to—"

"Come on, Lucy, cut the stories and answer the question. Did you see anyone around?"

"No."

"Lucy," Hawkeye asked, "did anyone else know about your party?"

"Ummm—yes."

"Who?" Hawkeye asked.

"Sarah."

Amy sighed. "Look, Lucy, you're not making our job any—"

Just then, Sarah Trippi skipped down the sidewalk to the Adams home. Lucy quickly filled Sarah in on what had taken place. Almost immediately, there was a double rerun of the crying scene.

"Whaaaaaaa!" Sarah shrieked. "My Smurfette and my Annie and my Tigger and my Softina and . . ."

Sarah's outburst got Lucy rolling again. "My Snoopy . . . my Cabbage Patch Kid . . . my Winnie the Pooh . . . my Baby Raspberry Tart . . . my Raggedy Ann . . ."

"You guys," Hawkeye hollered above the crying, "cut it out! Amy and I will get your dolls and animals back. We *promise*. But no more crying, OK?"

The girls snuffed, sniffled, coughed, and hiccupped their way back to silence.

"Sarah," Amy asked, "did anyone besides you and Lucy know about the tea party?"

"Yup."

"Who?"

"My mom and dad. But I don't think they'd kidnap my dolls."

"Of course they wouldn't, Sarah. What I meant was other people, other kids."

Sarah concentrated for a moment, unconsciously picking at a scab on the back of her hand. Suddenly, she began jumping up and down, waving her arms. "I've got it! It was Darth Vader! I *know* it was! He's the only one mean enough to do it. And he's big enough to carry all the dolls and animals. There were a million of them."

"Six—" Amy began, then caught herself. "Hawkeye," she said, "I can't take any more interviewing. Let's have a look out back."

"Right," Hawkeye said, pulling his sketch pad from the back pocket of his jeans. "But shouldn't we call the FBI first?"

"Call the president! Call the president!" Sarah shouted. "He'll help—my dad voted for him!"

"No, no! Call Mr. Rogers," Lucy demanded. "He doesn't have a job, so he won't be busy. He doesn't know I don't watch his show anymore."

"Nice going, Hawkeye," Amy whispered. "Next, we'll be watching the National Guard set up camp."

Hawkeye grinned at her. "Come on, guys," he said. "Let's take a look at the scene of the kidnapping."

Amy and Hawkeye led the way, followed by Lucy and Sarah.

"Keep off the dirt until I finish my sketch." Hawkeye's pencil raced across the page, his inquisitive artist's eyes flicking back and forth between the picnic table, the dirt, the benches, and then back to his sketch pad. In a few moments, his drawing was finished.

"See if you two can solve this case from my sketch," Hawk-eye told the little girls.

"Tough case, isn't it, Amy?" Hawkeye said.

"A bear," Amy answered with a smile, "a real bear."

Hawkeye tore the page from his sketch pad and handed it to Sarah. Lucy moved close to her friend, and they concentrated on the drawing. "See if you two can solve this case from my sketch," Hawkeye said.

"It was two snakes!" Sarah said. "See those marks? Snakes could've made them."

"No, Sarah, it wasn't snakes," Hawkeye said.

"It must have been a whole bunch of kids to carry all those dolls and animals," Lucy said.

"No, Lucy, I doubt it," Amy said. "Try a little harder. We've got a good hunch about who did this kidnapping."

HOW DID HAWKEYE AND AMY KNOW WHO THE KIDNAPPER WAS?

See page 77

The Case of the Fisherman's Favorite

For once, Sergeant Treadwell didn't greet his friends Amy Adams and Hawkeye Collins with his familiar, broad smile. Instead, he slumped glumly in the chair behind his desk. His usually active hands lay folded in his lap.

Hawkeye's sharp eyes immediately noticed that Sarge's desktop held only police communications, wanted posters, and the paperwork that made up a major part of Sarge's work for the Lakewood Hills Police Department.

What was missing was food. Sarge was addicted to snacking. It was very unusual to find him at his desk without a bag of pretzels, hard candy, potato chips, or popcorn—whatever junk food struck his fancy when he stopped at the grocery store on West Street every morning on his way to work.

Amy also noticed the lack of munchies on Sarge's desk. She realized that Sarge hadn't been at the ice cream shop for his Monday hot fudge sundae—and Sarge dearly loved hot fudge sundaes. Amy's mother, a doctor, had told Sarge to cut down to two sundaes per week: one on Monday, and one on Friday. Since Amy had never known him to skip one before, she was worried. And she could tell from Hawkeye's look of concern that, once again, they were practically reading each other's mind.

"Sit down, Amy, Hawkeye. Thanks for coming. I appreciate it. I . . . I can't go to the other officers on the force with this case. It's too . . . delicate . . . too embarrassing. I can't tell them I took such poor care of something they gave me. If you two can't crack this one, I just don't know what I'll do. I feel like a class-A fool." Sarge let his sentence trail off into silence. Even his voice had lost its usual lively tone.

"What's the matter, Sarge?" Hawkeye asked. "You look like your best friend just picked your pocket. What can we do for you?"

Amy's voice was quiet and concerned. "Do you feel OK, Sarge? Do you want me to give Mom a call?"

"No, Amy," Sarge answered, "I don't feel

well—not well at all. But I'm afraid your mom can't help. I'm not physically sick. I just wish it were that easy."

Hawkeye leaned forward in his chair. "How about starting at the beginning and filling us in? I know I really don't have to say this, but anything you tell Amy and me in this office stays right here. Now, what's the problem?"

Sarge sighed and shifted in his chair. "Remember when I lectured on crime prevention at your school last Thursday? Well, my squad car was at Sam's Service Station, getting a tune-up, so I drove my own car. You know the one I mean, Hawkeye: the station wagon you call the barge." A reference to his car's nickname usually brought a chuckle from Sarge, but not this time.

"Anyway, I parked in the teachers' lot behind your school. As usual, I locked my car. What I didn't realize at the time was that I'd rolled down the window of the tailgate and had forgotten to put it up again. My beautiful, handmade fly-fishing rod—the one the guys gave me on my twenty-fifth anniversary with the LHPD—was in the back of my station wagon. When I came back to the car after the lecture, my rod was gone—stolen.

"Of course, the rod was insured. But money can't replace something like that. The man who makes the rods is a real craftsman, only finishing a couple of them a year. The thought and effort

13

behind a present like that simply can't be bought and paid for. I'll feel terrible if the guys find out how careless I was with their gift."

Sarge hesitated for a long moment, cleared his throat, and then went on with his story. "Another thing," he said, "is that I believed the kids at Lakewood Hills Elementary School were my friends. Now I wonder. Sure, no one had any reason to think the wagon was mine—most of the kids have never even seen it. Still, to steal something right after my lecture on crime prevention—that really hurts."

"You're *not* wrong about the kids, Sarge—not at all," said Amy. "The kids *are* your friends."

"Yeah," Hawkeye added, "Amy's right. Think back to what you've taught us, Sarge. In almost every large group of people, there are one or two with sticky fingers or the urge to turn a quick, dishonest dollar. As you said, it's unfortunate, but it's a fact of life."

"Sarge," Amy asked, "was there anything about the rod that would prove it's yours? A serial number or something?"

"Nothing but a brass cap on the end of the rod with my initials on it. And that could be removed very easily."

Hawkeye was staring off into space, his thoughts apparently a million miles away from Sergeant Treadwell's office.

"Hawkeye?" Amy said. No response.

14

"Hawkeye!" she repeated irritably. "Have you been listening?"

Hawkeye returned to earth. "Yes, I've been listening. And I've got a problem. You know Sammy Jackson, the new kid who just moved into town? He lives out on Summer Avenue in the house the Stuart family sold."

Amy's face became tense with concentration. "Sammy Jackson . . . Sammy Jackson . . . oh, yeah! The kid from Rochester, New York. His sister's trying out for the track team. But what bothers you about Sammy?"

"Just this: Sammy asked me to go fishing last Friday—the day after Sarge's rod was stolen."

Amy paled. "You don't think . . . ?"

"I don't think *anything*, Amy. Maybe—probably—Sammy just likes to fish."

"Hawkeye's right," said Sarge. "If a person wants to go fishing, that certainly doesn't mean he or she is a crook."

Hawkeye checked his digital watch, then stood up. "Sarge," he said, "we'll do everything we can. We know how important that fly rod is to you. We'll ask some questions around school, but we won't make a big deal out of it. If some kid did take the rod, he or she may ditch it if our sleuthing is too obvious. I'm going to ride my bike over to Sammy's house right now—just to drop in and talk about fishing."

Amy rose from her chair and walked around

the desk. She put her hand on Sarge's shoulder and kissed the bald spot on the top of his head. "We'll get your rod back, Sarge," she promised. "After all, as far as solving mysteries goes, we've had the best teacher in the world—you."

At that, Sarge finally managed a smile.

Hawkeye pedaled up the driveway at 222 Summer Avenue—the Jackson home.

A trim, pleasant woman in her middle forties answered Hawkeye's knock at the front door.

"Hi," Hawkeye said. "Are you Mrs. Jackson?" The lady smiled and nodded. "I'm Christopher Collins—but people call me Hawkeye. I'm a friend of Sammy's."

"Oh, yes," replied Mrs. Jackson, "Hawkeye Collins. Sammy has talked about you. He hopes you're as crazy about fishing as he is. I swear Sammy would rather catch a three-pound bass than get a lifetime pass at the Video Arcade. He's in the basement fiddling with his fishing gear."

"Hey, Hawkeye," Sammy said with a grin as Hawkeye came down the stairs, "I'm really glad you stopped by. I've got something to show you— a brand-new rod! Feels like I've been saving for it forever, but I finally got the loot together. Here—take a look at this beauty!" And Sammy held out the fishing rod.

All the tension left Hawkeye in a great whoosh of a sigh. He laughed as he took the rod from his new friend. "This *is* a beauty, Sammy! It's as light as a feather. And the action—wow! You'll clean out Loon Lake with this baby. When I see a spinning rod like this, I wonder why anyone bothers with a fly rod."

"Right," Sammy agreed. "I've tried fly-fishing once or twice, but it didn't do much for me. I just couldn't get excited about it."

"Have you broken in your new rod yet?"

"Nope," answered Sammy. "How about Saturday morning, early?"

"Great!" Hawkeye said. "I'm not an expert, but I've gone fishing with my uncle and my dad a few times, and I really liked it. I've got to move now, Sammy, but let's plan on Saturday for sure!"

The next morning, Hawkeye was running a few minutes late. As he leaned over the combination lock of his locker in the hall at Lakewood Hills Elementary, Macho Thornton—big, mean, and always looking for trouble—slammed his own locker door against Hawkeye's shoulder.

"Are you going to be a meatball *all* your life, Macho? How about growing up?"

"I'm so sorry," Macho said sarcastically. "I hope I didn't hurt you, James Bond—or is it Thomas Magnum this week?"

Hawkeye, pulling books from his locker, pretended to ignore Macho. Then casually, almost as an afterthought, he said, "Macho, why don't the two of us go fishing next Saturday? Maybe if we got to know each other, we'd get along better. What do you say?"

Macho's eyes narrowed to slits. "What makes you think I'd want to spend any time with a creep like you? Anyway, I don't have fishing stuff—hooks and poles and all that crud. I've never been fishing in my life, and I don't want to start now. You're wasting time trying to get on my good side, Collins. I don't need junior cops for friends."

As Macho turned back to his locker, his hand hit the door, and he dropped the books and papers he was carrying. He tried to cover one scrap of paper with his foot as he fumbled with the other items he'd dropped. His face reddened, and he grabbed hurriedly and clumsily for his things. As he snatched at them, he ripped the paper beneath his shoe. Not even noticing the scrap of paper still on the floor, Macho stood up and hurried down the hall toward the sixth-grade classroom, elbowing and shoving students out of his way.

Hawkeye picked up the paper scrap, stuffed it into his pocket, and hurried off to his classroom. One thing he definitely did not need, Hawkeye thought, was another discussion with the principal about tardiness.

It seemed like hours before Mr. Bronson, the sixth-grade teacher, turned his back to the class as he worked a math problem on the board. Hawkeye took the scrap of paper from his pocket and

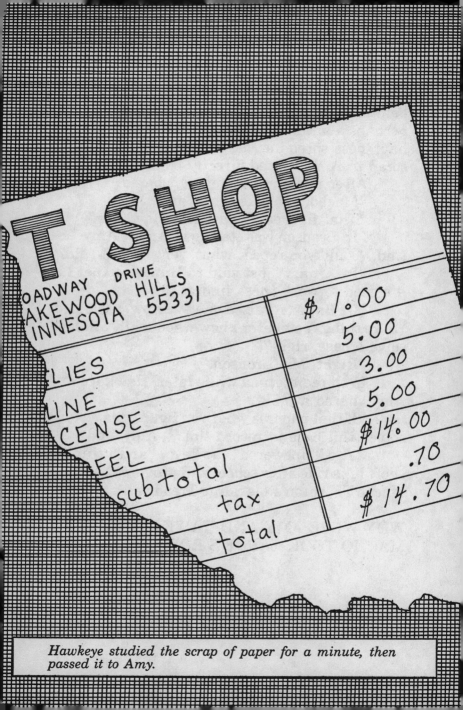

T SHOP

OADWAY   DRIVE
AKEWOOD HILLS
INNESOTA 55331

	$ 1.00
	5.00
LIES	3.00
LINE	5.00
CENSE	$ 14.00
EEL	
subtotal	.70
tax	$ 14.70
total	

Hawkeye studied the scrap of paper for a minute, then passed it to Amy.

smoothed it neatly on the top of his desk, behind his math book. He studied the scrap for perhaps a minute. Then a grin of both relief and happiness spread across his face. He passed the scrap to Amy, seated directly behind him.

After a moment, Amy whispered, "Who?"

"Macho," Hawkeye whispered back.

"That figures. Good work, Hawkeye."

Mr. Bronson was staring at Amy. "Amy," he said, "could you repeat whatever you just said?"

"I . . . uh. . . just said to Hawkeye that . . . it's good to work these figures."

Mr. Bronson raised one eyebrow, then said, "Sure thing. You never know when math will help solve a case, right?"

"Right, Mr. Bronson."

In the cafeteria a while later, Hawkeye and Amy shared a table.

"If that paper is what you figure it is, you've solved this case in record time," Amy said.

"Yep," answered Hawkeye, "and I think a short bike ride after school will prove we're right: Macho Thornton stole Sarge Treadwell's fly rod!"

WHY WERE AMY AND HAWKEYE SO SURE MACHO TOOK SARGE'S ROD?

See page 81

The Case of the Toilet Paper Decorator

Hawkeye Collins, Amy Adams, and Sergeant Treadwell stood gawking at the mess in Mr. Bronson's yard. All three of them had been by the sixth-grade teacher's home hundreds, and in Sarge's case thousands, of times. But never before had the yard and house—every bush, tree, and roof peak—been completely decorated with toilet paper.

"Wow!" Hawkeye managed to croak.

Amy shifted her feet in the dew-soaked grass in Mr. Bronson's front yard. For once, at least momentarily, she was without words.

Sarge waved his hand toward the house.

"Have you ever seen anything like that before?" he asked, irritation making his voice louder than necessary. "This is why I dragged you two over here at eight o'clock on a Saturday morning. I need your skills. I want whoever did this to learn that they've gone too far. A little T.P. is funny for Halloween, maybe, but this is a cruel practical joke."

"Sarge," Amy said quietly, putting her hand lightly on his arm, "you're . . . uh . . . shouting. We know you're upset, but please try to calm down."

"Now," Hawkeye said, "how about filling us in on what you know about this?"

Sergeant Treadwell took several deep breaths to calm himself before he spoke.

"OK. As you know, Lakewood Hills was without power for slightly over two hours last night, after the tornado dumped a tree on the main generator line. So, no lights. No streetlights, no store lights, no traffic lights—no lights of any kind. That happened at exactly 7:08 P.M.

"At 8:15, Mel Stevens—you know, the power company's chief lineman—was driving down Water Street to get to a downed power line. The poor guy was out all night, clearing the main lines as well as he was able. Anyway, as I said, Mel was coming down Water Street at 8:15. His headlights picked up someone running across the street, away from Mr. Bronson's yard. Then he saw the house and got on the radio to me."

"This person running across Water Street—

could Mel give you an ID?" Amy asked.

Sarge sighed. "Yes and no. Mel said the person was a youngster, and he thinks that youngster may have been Macho Thornton."

"How sure is Mel, Sarge? Can he swear to what he saw?" Hawkeye asked.

"That's the problem," Sarge replied. "He can't. He said the guy's size and hair and clothing looked right, but there was so much blowing dirt and debris that he can't swear the person he saw was Macho. And, as you two know, a witness who 'thinks' he or she saw someone or something isn't much use to us."

"We'll talk to Macho," Hawkeye said.

"Good. He'll probably—no, definitely—be more open with you than he was with me this morning. He seemed scared stiff when he opened the door. Of course, that's nothing new. Macho looks scared stiff *every* time he sees me."

"What about other evidence?" Amy asked.

"None," Sarge answered. "There was just too much blowing going on. Amy, Hawkeye, I'll ask you to take the investigation from here."

The worried frown on Macho Thornton's face was replaced with a wide, beaming smile as he responded to the knocking on his front door and found the two sleuths on the porch.

"Amy! Hawkeye!" he exclaimed. "Come on in, ol' buddies! Boy, a guy really finds out who his true friends are when there's a little trouble, right? I was just thinking—right before you knocked— that my chums Hawkeye and Amy wouldn't let me down."

Amy rolled her eyes. Hawkeye got down to business.

"Did you decorate Mr. Bronson's house, Macho?"

"No! I didn't do it—I give you my word! And I'm afraid Fatwell—'scuse me, I mean Sergeant Treadwell—is trying to frame me just 'cause I've been in a little trouble once or twice before."

"Where were you at 8:15 last night?" Amy asked.

"I was here at home all night. I was listening to my Walkman. Practically wore out the batteries. When the lights went out, I lit one of our camping lanterns. My folks were in Minneapolis, visiting friends. They couldn't get back home until this morning 'cause of the storm and all the downed power lines."

"So you were alone all night?" Hawkeye asked.

"Yeah. Sergeant Treadwell woke me by rapping on the door this morning. Look: I didn't do it. You two know I ain't bright enough to come up with a neat idea like that, don't you?"

"Good point, Macho," Amy said.

"That reminds me, Macho. How did you do on the social studies test this week?"

Hawkeye asked. "Did you pass?"

"Bronson gave me an *F*, the turkey." Macho's eyes widened. "But you don't think that's why I—I mean, I didn't, but you don't think I was getting back at Bronson, do you?"

Hawkeye stared directly into Macho's eyes. Macho looked back at him, then said, "Honest, Hawkeye, it wasn't me. I'm innocent."

Macho put his right hand on Amy's shoulder and his left on Hawkeye's. "Can you get your pal Macho off? You *do* believe me, don't you?"

Hawkeye and Amy turned to one another. Their eyes met and locked. After a long moment, Amy looked at Macho.

"We believe you, Macho," she said, "although I'm not quite sure why. I don't know whether we can get you off the hook, though."

"We'll do our best," Hawkeye added. "But keep in mind that Sarge Treadwell is hot on this case, and you're a prime suspect. You'd better stick close to home today."

"Sure, partners," Macho agreed.

Amy and Hawkeye walked slowly away from Macho's house.

Amy snorted in disgust. "If that turkey had called us 'pals,' 'buddies,' 'partners,' or 'friends' one more time, I would have barfed on his boots."

"Yeah," Hawkeye said, "but I think we both have the gut feeling that Macho's innocent. Plus, he's not smart enough to be a good liar. Let's discuss what we have—maybe something will lead to something else."

"OK," Amy said. "We know the house was T.P.'d about 8:15, during the blackout. Mel Stevens can't make a positive ID of Macho. Say . . . you know, Bad News Thomas is roughly the same size as Macho, and this type of vandalism is more like Bad News' style. I wonder . . ."

Hawkeye shook his head dubiously. "That's weak, Amy—lots of kids are Macho's size and build. Still, a weak lead is better than no lead at all. Let's take a walk over to his house and have a talk with Bad News."

It took Bad News Thomas several moments to answer the door. During that short time, Hawkeye tugged his sketch pad from the back pocket of his jeans. The door swung open.

"Well," Bad News said, "if it ain't the Dynamic Duo: Batbrain and Rubberhead."

"Nice to see you, too, Bad News," Hawkeye said evenly.

Bad News squinted his eyes in anger. "You junior detectives are pulling your James Bond routine about Bronson's house, right? I just heard about it on the radio. You've come to the wrong place. I was home all night, reading. I went to bed at 9:30."

"Who else was here with you?" Amy asked.

"Not that it's any of your business, Lois Lane, but I was alone until almost 10:00, when my

"I'm sure there's some key clue in this sketch," said Amy.

parents got home. They were playing bridge with the Goldmans, just two houses down. They played cards by candlelight—the same way I read. When the power went off, I lit a candle, sat in that easy chair, and read some old comics. Look—there's the candle, the chair, and the comics, right there."

"Hmm," Amy said. "I thought you'd be doing makeup homework to get out of your *F* in social studies. Aren't you on probation?"

Hawkeye stood slightly behind and to the side of Amy, his pencil flying furiously over the surface of the sketch pad page.

"I got nothin' else to say to you creeps," Bad News snarled. He slammed the door.

Hawkeye handed his drawing to Amy, and she studied it as they walked toward home.

"You're getting faster, Hawkeye," she said. "This is a really nice piece of work. I'm sure there's something . . . some key clue . . . in this sketch. I hate to admit it, but Bad News' story seems sound enough. Still, I—"

"Hey!" Hawkeye exploded. "Take a closer look at the sketch, Amy! Bad News lied about his alibi—and I bet he lied about the T.P., too!"

WHAT SHOWED THAT BAD NEWS HAD LIED?

See page 83

The Mystery of the Furry Lifesaver

Hawkeye Collins sat at the breakfast table and reread the headline and front-page story of the Sunday *Lakewood Hills Herald*:

MYSTERY DOG SAVES LIFE
OF LOCAL TODDLER

An unidentified dog saved the life of Stanley Terhune, of 497 Summer Avenue, about 2:30 yesterday afternoon. Three-year-old Stanley, who had accompanied his mother to the monthly meeting of the Lakewood Hills Women for Peace Coalition, apparently wandered away from the meeting site on the patio of La Cuisine Restaurant and found his way to the end of the dock on Loon Lake. It is believed that he then toppled into the water and was forced under the surface by the high waves that resulted from yesterday's strong winds.

It was then that the heroic canine averted what could very easily have become a tragedy. The dog either swam from the shore or jumped from the dock to reach Stanley. The toddler must have grasped the dog's collar instinctively and clung to it while the dog swam to shore.

Steven Ruffino, 16, of 275 Maple Street, was on the beach when the incident occurred. Blind since birth, Ruffino followed the sound of Stanley's cries to the spot where the dog brought the child ashore.

"I wish I could help identify the dog, but I can't," said Ruffino at the scene. "I felt the dog's fur and its leather collar, but then I just concentrated on keeping the kid calm and getting help."

Ruffino refused to accept any reward for his part in the rescue. "I didn't do anything," he protested. "If there is any reward, it should go to the dog or its owner. That dog is a real hero."

Mrs. Terhune has offered a fifty-dollar gift to the owner of the dog as a "token to its heroism."

Hawkeye snapped his fingers. He looked at his golden retriever, sprawled on the kitchen floor. "Come here, Nosey," he said.

Nosey thumped her tail against the floor, rose, and trotted to Hawkeye's side. She stood there, looking expectantly at her master.

Hawkeye scratched behind Nosey's ears and gently stroked her head.

"Hmmm," he mused aloud. Nosey wagged her tail.

When class started the next morning in the Lakewood Hills Elementary School sixth grade, Margaret Mason raised her hand to get the teacher's attention. As she did so, the bright morning sun glittered off the diamond ring she wore. Margaret's father owned a fleet of coal barges on the Mississippi River. Next to Mrs. von Buttermore, he was the wealthiest person in Lakewood Hills. Margaret was very, very conscious of her parents' money and social position.

"Mr. Bronson," Margaret said, "I'm sure you've read yesterday's *Herald*. I just wanted to say that my magnificent boxer, Cash, is the mystery dog that saved the little kid. None of the mutts in town could have done what Cash did—they just don't have his breeding. I don't care about the reward, but I want to make sure everybody knows it was Cash."

Hawkeye heard Amy squirming at the desk directly behind him. He sighed—he knew better than to try to quiet her. Amy and Margaret had always disliked each other.

Mr. Bronson nodded toward Amy's wildly waving hand.

"I don't think," Amy said, "a dog's value comes just from its breeding. There are plenty of fine, brave dogs in Lakewood Hills, and some of them are mutts. Also, I doubt very much that Cash is the mystery dog."

Margaret laughed. "I suppose *you* know who the mystery dog is."

"Yes, I do!" Amy said heatedly.

"Don't tell me it's your dog, Bernie!" Margaret rolled her eyes. "Who ever heard of a St. Bernard swimming!"

"Oh, boy, here it comes!" Hawkeye mumbled to himself.

"No—it's Nosey—Hawkeye Collins' golden retriever. She's the dog that saved Stanley Terhune!"

Heads turned toward Amy, and whispers buzzed throughout the classroom.

"Prove it, turkey!" snapped Margaret.

"I will prove it! And who are you calling a—"

"Class! Class!" Mr. Bronson called. "Come to order! I'm sure both Cash and Nosey are fine dogs. But this isn't the time or the place to discuss the subject. Now . . . please open your history texts."

Amy and Hawkeye sat across from each other at a table in the cafeteria. Amy sipped her milk, but left her sandwich almost untouched.

"Hawkeye," Amy said, "I just know Nosey saved little Stanley. I'm *positive* of it. You know how much Nosey loves water, and you know she swims as often as she can near La Cuisine. That's proof—"

"But that's just it," Hawkeye cut in. "It *isn't* proof—and it isn't evidence, either. I wondered when I read the story if it'd been Nosey. But we just can't tell. I hate to say it, but you may have stuck both your feet in your mouth this morning. Sure, Margaret is a royal pain sometimes, but it's still possible that Cash—"

"Come on, Hawkeye," Amy said, irritation clear in her voice. "Cash is about as bright as a brick. Remember how he found the dead skunk in the road and dragged it into Mrs. Mason's dinner party? Remember how he held Sarge at bay and let that prowler escape from the Mason's house? That beast is a four-footed moron."

Hawkeye had taken his sketch pad from his back pocket as Amy spoke.

"Hawkeye! Are you listening?"

"Uh . . . yeah . . . sure, I'm listening. I'm just fooling around while I think."

Amy's green eyes flashed with impatience. "Look, I still think Nosey saved the kid. Will you ride out to La Cuisine with me after school? I want to look around."

"OK. Amy, you know I think it's possible that Nosey saved Stanley. But let's not go barging in on this thing, or else we'll look as foolish as Margaret, making claims we can't back up."

"Fine. But I sure hope we can prove our hunch. I'd *love* rubbing dear, sweet Margaret's nose in her stupid bragging."

Amy, legs pumping the pedals of her ten-speed like pistons, was 20 yards ahead of Hawkeye when they reached La Cuisine. They had swung by Hawkeye's house to pick up Nosey. The golden retriever bounded along at Hawkeye's side as he struggled, red-faced, to overtake Amy. He was going to lose still another bike race to her.

Margaret Mason had had the same idea of visiting the scene of the rescue and had Cash on a leash near the dock. Her father's chauffeur-driven limousine waited for her near the front door of the restaurant.

Irene Detmore, the receptionist at La Cuisine, waved at Amy and Hawkeye from the patio in front of the restaurant. "Lots of excitement here yesterday," she called.

"There sure was," Amy answered. "Irene, did you see Nosey around here—or down on the beach or dock—on Saturday?"

"No, I didn't," Irene answered, "but that doesn't mean anything. I was inside all day, preparing the main dining room for a banquet. I didn't even know about Stanley until the rescue squad arrived. He's one lucky kid—the lake was really rolling that day."

Hawkeye and Amy wandered about the patio area, then walked out onto the dock. They weren't looking for anything in particular; they were just looking. Loon Lake was calm, but the water still looked muddy from the wind and waves of the days before.

Mrs. Terhune was sitting on a beach towel, pouring herself a cup of coffee from a thermos. She was keeping a very close watch on little Stanley, who was playing with a toy truck in the sand.

"Hi, kids," she said. "I thought some dog owners would be out here today, so I drove down to make good on my reward offer. I wish it could be much, much more—but I wanted to do something so that the dog gets the credit he or she deserves."

Margaret, dragging the uncooperative Cash by his leash, approached Mrs. Terhune. Their classmate ignored Amy and Hawkeye.

"I," she said, "am Margaret Mason. This boxer is the hero dog—the dog that saved your son's life. Please make the check payable to—"

"Now just a minute, Margaret," Amy said angrily. "Let's take the dogs over to Stanley—maybe he can help somehow."

Margaret looked worried—or angry—but she saw no way to refuse what Amy had proposed. She began hauling her dog toward the boy.

"Hawkeye," Amy said, "while we do that, could you quickly sketch the dogs?"

Hawkeye tugged his sketch pad from his back pocket and went to work.

Stanley Terhune pushed himself to his feet and waved his chubby arms.

"Doggy! Doggy!" he said, grabbing one of Nosey's ears with his left hand and clobbering her face happily with his right. Nosey licked his face, her tail whipping back and forth as Stanley giggled between slurps.

Margaret, meanwhile, was pulling on the leash with all her strength to drag Cash over to Stanley.

Stanley noticed Cash and started toward him, arms out. " 'Nother doggy!" he said. " 'Nother doggy!" Cash froze, his eyes widening, and the hair rose along his spine. Quickly, Amy grabbed

Hawkeye pulled his sketch pad from his back pocket and quickly drew the two dogs.

Stanley's arm and led him toward his mother. "Friendly pooch you have there, Margaret. He must *love* kids—for dinner."

Hawkeye handed his sketch pad to Amy. She studied it for several moments, winked at Hawkeye, and then handed the pad to Mrs. Terhune.

"I bet Hawkeye will agree with me on this, Mrs. Terhune," Amy said. "Unless someone provides absolute proof that another dog is the hero, you may want to make your reward check payable to the National Blindness Research Foundation. We can't positively prove that Nosey saved Stanley, but if you'll take a good, close look at Hawkeye's sketch, you'll see why Cash couldn't be the hero dog."

WHAT SHOWED AMY THAT CASH WAS NOT THE HERO DOG?

See page 85

The Case of the Suspicious Soybeans

Hawkeye Collins and Amy Adams practiced no-hands riding on their ten-speeds as they rode down Lakeside Drive toward Mrs. von Buttermore's mansion on Loon Lake. It was a cool, crystal-clear September afternoon—the type of day that would have driven the two sixth graders right up the wall if it had been a school day. Fortunately, it was a Saturday, and the glorious weather was theirs to enjoy.

Mrs. von Buttermore, easily the most wealthy person in Lakewood Hills, had invited Amy and Hawkeye to her mansion for afternoon tea, and to meet a man she described as "a great humanitarian and a loving human being."

"Hawkeye," Amy asked, "are you *positive* you got this fellow's name right when Mrs. von Buttermore called you this morning?"

"Absolutely, Amy. I even asked her to repeat it to me. His name *is* Starshine Goodhealth. In fact, Mrs. von Buttermore told me his full name is Starshine Peacelove Goodhealth."

Amy mulled that over for several moments. "I wonder," she asked, "what kind of parents would hang a name like that on their kid? It's awful!"

"I asked my dad the same question," Hawkeye replied. "He told me that during the sixties, the hippies very often dropped their actual names and called themselves all sorts of weird things. He said that during the 'flower power' days, there were lots of people named Peace N. Love. Those people thought that changing their names would make everybody stop fighting and get along with each other."

"How could changing your name to Peace N. Love make other people stop fighting?" Amy asked.

"Beats me," replied Hawkeye as they swung their bikes onto Mrs. von Buttermore's winding driveway.

Hawkeye and Amy left their ten-speeds on the lawn near the front door of the mansion and stood gaping at the van parked next to the house. It was completely covered with fluorescent, eye-searing pictures of flowers, sunsets, and mountain scenes, over which were scrawled various slogans: "I Love You," "Flower Power," "Can You Dig Me?" and "Keep on Truckin'."

"A real peaceful-looking machine, huh?" Amy commented with a smirk on her face.

"Yeah."

Mrs. von Buttermore opened the front door just as Amy was about to knock.

"Amy, Hawkeye! I'm so glad to see you! Please come in and meet Starshine—he's *such* a beautiful person!" Mrs. von Buttermore led the way to the library. Behind her, Hawkeye and Amy exchanged confused looks. Neither had seen their older friend in such a state before. While a kind, loving, and intelligent person, she had always been the very picture of a genteel, composed sixty-year-old lady.

"Hawkeye, Amy," she said as she stepped into her huge, impressive library, "please say hello to Starshine Peacelove Goodhealth."

A slender, well-tanned man of about forty stood in the center of the room. His brownish blond hair was pulled back into a ponytail, which hung well below his waist. Each of his pierced ears glittered with small jewels attached to silver chains. He wore a buckskin jacket with foot-long fringes on the sleeves, and faded but clean jeans. He was barefoot.

"I love you," Starshine said to a surprised Hawkeye and Amy.

41

"Uh . . . yeah . . . right," Hawkeye answered.

For once, Amy was without words.

Mrs. von Buttermore seated the somewhat dazed sixth graders. "Starshine," she said, "appeared at my door three days ago. When he first explained his plan to me, I must admit that I was a bit skeptical. But when I learned that Starshine would make no profit, and that his plan is based on his love for all people, I became a believer."

"Uh . . . plan, Mrs. von Buttermore?" Hawkeye asked.

Starshine walked over to Mrs. von Buttermore and put his hand gently on her shoulder. "This lovely lady is going to help me to do two things for the good of all humanity. We're going to feed all the hungry people in the world—*all* of them—and help to abolish the uncivilized, unhealthy, barbaric custom of eating meat. I personally have not eaten meat in any form since June 3, 1962, and I'm in perfect health. I haven't been sick for a minute: no colds, no flu, nothing. It's meat that's destroying the health of our planet's people."

Neither Hawkeye nor Amy said a word. Starshine looked from one to the other, then continued.

"The food of the future, the food that will save the human race, is the soybean. Soybeans provide morc protein, fiber, vitamins, and minerals per ounce than any meat. A vegetarian way of life—combining soybeans with fresh fruits, vegetables, and grain, and eating no meat whatsoever—will guarantee both vibrant good health and a long life.

"Furthermore, soybeans can be grown just about anywhere,"—he opened his arms wide—"and a single acre of soybeans can feed hundreds of people. The beans can be ground for bread or combined with various grains for soups or gruel. The possibilities are limitless."

"No meat?" Amy asked.

"No, Amy, none. None at all. Humans don't have the right to murder and eat animals!"

"I . . . uh . . . don't mean to be rude, Mr. . . . uh . . . Goodhealth, but I doubt that the calf your jacket came from donated its hide."

Starshine sighed deeply. "You're correct, Amy—absolutely correct. But one day, while I was in deep meditation, a voice told me to dress myself in the skins of animals in order to glorify the beauty of all animals. I've done so ever since then."

"The plan, Starshine," Mrs. von Buttermore said eagerly, "tell them about the plan!"

"It's quite simple," Starshine said. "I've purchased a thousand acres of land in Kansas—or rather, I *will* purchase it with the help of this lady—which will be planted with soybeans. Then the harvest will be given away to all who need it. At the same time, I'll spread the tragic truth about what eating meat is doing to the health of the people of the world."

Hawkeye asked, "Where does Mrs. von Buttermore fit into your plan?"

"Ahhh, yes," Starshine replied. "Dear, loving Mrs. von Buttermore. She will be helping to end world hunger with some . . . financial assistance."

Hawkeye leaned forward. "How much—"

Starshine cut Hawkeye off in midquestion. "The amount isn't impor—"

"Only a hundred thousand dollars at first," Mrs. von Buttermore interrupted, "but later . . ."

Both Amy and Hawkeye paled.

"I'm *so* glad to have met you," Starshine said abruptly, "but this lady and I have much to discuss. Please feel free to visit me at the Lakebreeze Motel if you care to make a donation."

"It smells," Hawkeye said later as he and Amy pedaled down the driveway to Lakeside Drive. "The whole thing smells. That guy's using Mrs. von Buttermore's kindness and generosity to line his own pockets. I *guarantee* it."

"I agree one hundred percent," Amy replied. "Our only problem is proving it."

Hawkeye nodded in agreement. "Look," he said, "let's ride back over this way to the Lakebreeze Motel after supper and have a little talk with that creep—alone."

Al Warren, desk clerk at the Lakebreeze Motel, greeted Hawkeye and Amy. "Hi, kids.

How've you both been?"

"Fine, Al, just fine," answered Amy. "We're here to see Mr. Goodhealth. Is he in?"

"Yeah, he is," Al said. "Number 206—one of the kitchenette units."

"Thanks, Al," Hawkeye said as he and Amy began walking across the lobby to the stairs. On the way, Hawkeye tugged his sketch pad out of his back pocket.

Amy knocked on the door of unit 206. After a few moments, Starshine Peacelove Goodhealth opened the door.

"Hawkeye! Amy! Hey, how's it going, guys? Hey, don't tell me why you came—you want to make a donation, right?"

"Well, not exactly," Amy said. "We'd like to talk over your plan. We have a few questions about it."

As Amy spoke, Hawkeye stood slightly behind her, his pencil racing over the page of his sketch pad. He recorded every detail his sharp eyes took in.

Amy cleared her throat, trying to stall. "Um, Hawkeye and I were just talking about your plan, and we wondered if you could show us . . . ah, show us where the land is in Kansas. You know, the land you want to buy?"

Starshine's eyes narrowed. "Some other time, guys, OK?" he said. "Right now, I'm meditating. See you both around. I love you." The door

"Holy cow—or soybean—Hawkeye! The man is a fraud!"

was shut in their faces, and they heard the slide bolt click into place.

"Case closed. Let's call Sarge, quick!" Hawkeye said triumphantly, snapping his sketch pad shut. "Let's get to a phone."

Amy hurried along with Hawkeye, bursting with curiosity. "What was it? What's the deal?"

"I'll give you thirty seconds to figure it out." Hawkeye grinned and tossed her the pad.

Amy studied the sketch without breaking stride. "Holy cow—or soybean—Hawkeye, we've got him! The man is a fraud, and he gave us the evidence to prove it!"

HOW DID HAWKEYE AND AMY KNOW THAT STARSHINE WAS A FRAUD?

See page 87

The Case of the Kidnapped Brain

The tension in the air at Lakewood Hills Elementary School almost crackled. The halls, the classrooms, and the cafeteria all buzzed with the news: Newton Pestle had been kidnapped.

Again and again, a question arose in hushed, worried conversations among teachers and students—why Newton?

Sure, Newton was a genius; he went to Lakewood Hills Elementary only to learn how to get along with kids. During IQ testing at the school, a special team had been brought in from the nearby Minneapolis Institute of Learning Research specifically to watch him and talk with him. Newton had quite simply blown them away. The team had no scale that could measure his intelligence.

When he was a fourth grader, Newton designed and built a computer that beat the International Chess Federation's computer in a series of one hundred chess games—with no losses. Then Newton played against his own invention and beat it thirty-three times in a row. During the thirty-fourth game, the computer burst into flames. Newton got up from his chair and walked away, muttering, "Check and mate."

Still, kidnapping a sixth grader who was a genius and who built computers didn't make sense. Newton, an only child, lived with his parents in a pleasant little house on Maple Street, south of the Lakedale Shopping Mall. His mother worked part time at the public library, and his father was a salesman for an office supplies company and traveled frequently in his work. The Pestle family was comfortable, but far from wealthy. A kidnapper just wouldn't pick Newton as a victim if he wanted a lot of ransom money.

Hawkeye Collins and Amy Adams sat with the rest of the sixth-grade class. Their eyes locked on the front of the room as Officer Ellis of the Lakewood Hills Police Department walked in and handed a folded note to Mr. Bronson, their teacher. Mr. Bronson read the note, nodded to Officer Ellis, and cleared his throat.

"Amy and Hawkeye, please go along with Officer Ellis. This has been cleared with your parents. If you want to, you may call home from the principal's office before you leave."

Both Hawkeye and Amy got up from their desks.

"That's OK, Mr. Bronson," Hawkeye said. "We're ready to go, right, Amy?"

Amy nodded. "Right. We don't need to call anyone, Mr. Bronson."

Officer Ellis drove the LHPD prowl car a bit faster than normal between the school and police headquarters—a distance of a few short blocks. Both sixth graders noticed that Officer Ellis had unsnapped the security strap that held her service revolver in its holster.

"What's this all—" Amy began.

"Sorry," the officer interrupted. "No questions and no conversation. Sergeant Treadwell will fill you in at his office."

Hawkeye and Amy exchanged nervous, confused looks. "Wow!" Hawkeye mouthed silently. Amy fidgeted uneasily, nibbling on her lower lip.

Sergeant Treadwell looked both grim and official as he sat behind his strangely clutter-free desk. A middle-aged, athletic-looking man in a gray business suit stood next to Sarge, holding a large manila envelope.

"Amy, Hawkeye," Sarge said, "this gentleman is Investigator Michael Auborn of the National Security Council. He asked that you two be brought in on this case even before I suggested it."

"National Security? Case? What case, Sarge?" asked a bewildered Hawkeye.

"The kidnapping of Newton Pestle," Investigator Auburn answered. "Please keep in mind that anything—and everything—we discuss in this office today is essential to the security of our country. Nothing is to go beyond these walls—*ever*. Is that completely understood?"

"Yes, sir," Amy and Hawkeye answered together.

"OK. Good. We—the Security Council—have heard about you two youngsters. You do excellent work. We're proud of you." Investigator Auburn allowed himself a brief smile.

"Now on to business. Frank Pestle, Newton's father, is an undercover agent for the federal government. Some—individuals—must have broken his cover. We assume they've kidnapped his son to force Mr. Pestle to give them certain information.

"We don't think Newton has been harmed—yet. We have to find him very quickly, but we have next to nothing to go on. Mr. Pestle found a tape of Newton's voice in his mailbox. It's a common brand of tape, available almost anywhere. There were no fingerprints. The voice on the tape is Newton's; we've verified that through voiceprints we have on record of all our people and their families. Sergeant Treadwell believes the tape can tell you far more than it's told us. That's why we've called you in to help us."

Sarge took a small cassette player from his drawer and placed it in the center of his desk. He also handed a sheet of paper to Amy and Hawkeye.

"I'll play the tape," he said, "and you can follow the words on the paper. You *know* Newton—we don't. If you're as clever now as you have been before, you may find the lead—the key—we're all missing."

"Sarge," Amy protested, "Newton's always been a loner. We don't really know him—at least, not in the way you seem to think we do. I don't think we—"

Sarge held up his hand. "We realize that, Amy. But you and Hawkeye have been in the same grade and class with Newton for six years—seven, counting kindergarten. That puts you way ahead of us. There's an answer in this tape. There *has* to be. A youngster as bright as Newton wouldn't just jabber if he had a chance to let us know where he is. Maybe—just maybe—you'll be able to dig out what he's saying. All we can ask is that you do your best. OK?"

"Of course we'll do our best, Sarge," Hawkeye said.

"Yeah," added Amy, "but we sure hope our best is good enough. Whether we understand him or not, Newton is still our friend."

Sarge pushed a button on the tape player, and Newton's voice filled the office.

"Officer Larson: Drop money in Loon Lake, or leave dough Monday in leakproof lockboxes. Only listen; don't make idiotic, lousy l—"

"That's enough, you twerp!" a rough male voice cut in suddenly. The tape played out silently to its end.

Hawkeye shook his head, as if in shock.

"I don't believe it! He didn't say *where* in Loon Lake, or whether the money in the lockboxes is to go in the lake, or even how much money—hey, I thought you said this wasn't a money case anyway! What gives?"

Amy's voice was shaky. "And who's Officer Larson? There's nobody on the force with that name. I'm afraid he's drugged," she said. "He must be. Newton never would've said 'dough,' either."

"No, Amy," Investigator Auborn said. "Our voice analysis equipment shows no sign of any type of drug. Newton was definitely all right when he made this tape."

Hawkeye began pacing about the office.

Amy held the typed transcript, studying it. "He's leaving out words, too—twice he forgot the word *the*. It almost sounds like a coded message ... hmm ... but it looks too random. There's no sequence."

"How about dropping every other word, or every third word—something like that?" Hawkeye suggested.

LAKEWOOD HILLS POLICE DEPARTMENT
150 West Street
Lakewood Hills, MN 55331

OFFICIAL TELEPHONE TRANSCRIPT

Date recorded _March 8, 1984_

Date Transcribed _March 8, 1984_

Message Taken By _Officer Ellis_

Text:

Boy's voice: "Officer Larson, Drop money in Loon Lake, or leave dough Monday in leakproof lockboxes. Only listen; don't make idiotic, lousy l——"

Man's voice, interrupting: "That's enough, you twerp."

Sound of movement, then tape goes blank for rest of cassette.

I hereby certify that the foregoing text is a faithful transcription of the conversation in question.

Louise Ellis, LHP   3-8-84

Officer's Signature   Date

"How about dropping every other word—something like that?" suggested Hawkeye.

"No . . . no, . . . " Amy murmured, deep in thought. "Newton seemed to be speaking just the slightest bit more slowly than he usually does . . . as if he were calculating, planning each letter or word, rather than . . . just . . . just— Hey! Sarge, I think I've got something! Look at this transcript! I think we may have found our kidnapped genius—thanks to the genius himself!"

WHAT DID AMY NOTICE THAT TOLD HER WHERE NEWTON WAS BEING KEPT?

See page 89

The Case of the Amusement Park Punks

The gaily painted roller coaster car groaned and clanked its way up the almost vertical incline of the Over-the-Falls ride at the Lakewood Hills Amusement Park.

"Scared, Hawkeye?" Amy Adams asked.

"Uh . . . no . . . I'm not . . . scared," Hawkeye Collins answered. His voice cracked halfway through the word *scared*.

"Then how come your knuckles are white?"

"I . . . uh . . ."

The rest of Hawkeye's response never came. The first car—the one in which the two sleuths were riding—had reached the peak of its climb, and it jolted to a stop for a moment. To Hawkeye, that moment lasted several centuries. He swallowed hard and looked down at the dusty park sprawled out far below him. He swallowed again. Amy giggled. Then the force of gravity took over. The little car edged its way over the top of the peak, rolled a few feet at a crawl—and then hurtled downward as if it had been fired out of a cannon. Amy squealed in delight as the speed of the car increased to what seemed an almost impossible rate.

"Ulp!" Hawkeye croaked. He stared straight ahead at the large, rusty-colored pool of water that seemed to be racing toward them. The car splashed into the pool at the end of the tracks, throwing a huge curl of water up on either side. The impact of the front of the speeding car forced a five-foot wall of water up over the passengers, and the ride ended.

Both Amy and Hawkeye were soaked. Her red hair hung in dripping, straggly strands, and his blond hair was plastered against his skull. Hawkeye turned his head from side to side for a moment, acting very confused. Then suddenly, he tugged off his glasses and wiped the water from both sides of the lenses with his finger. Finally he and Amy climbed out of the car, onto the platform next to the pool.

"Thanks, Mr. Clemens—that was a gas," Amy called to the ride operator.

On the way to the hot dog stand, they passed

a set of funny mirrors. They glanced at themselves in one, and they both began to laugh.

"Now I know where the expression 'looking like a drowned rat' came from," Hawkeye gasped through his laughter.

"Right!" Amy agreed. "We couldn't have gotten wetter—"

The buzzing and crackling of the loudspeaker system cut into Amy's sentence.

"Hawkeye Collins and Amy Adams. Please report to Sergeant Treadwell at the ticket booth. I repeat . . ."

"What in the world is Sarge doing here?" Amy asked.

"Beats me," Hawkeye said, "but we'd better get over there and find out what he wants. It could be a case. I wonder how he knew we were here?"

"Sarge doesn't miss much," Amy replied, already breaking into a trot toward the ticket booth. "Remember, late last week we told him we were planning on coming here tonight because there's no school tomorrow?"

"Yeah," Hawkeye said. "I *do* remember, now that you mention it." He trotted alongside Amy.

Hawkeye and Amy had worked with Sergeant Treadwell of the Lakewood Hills Police Department on many cases. The friendly, middle-aged cop had been their number-one fan ever since they solved the theft of his own special fly rod.

Sergeant Treadwell was standing to one side of the ticket booth, next to a scruffy-looking guy about 16 or 17. Two other youths, about the same age as the first one and dressed like him in dirty, patched jeans, down-at-the-heel shoes, and stained T-shirts, stood a few feet away. All three were grimy and dusty, and it was obvious they'd been in the park area for at least a couple of hours.

Hell's Angels, Hawkeye thought to himself. Then he noticed that the young man next to Sarge had his hands behind his back.

Sarge looked grim. "Hello, Amy, Hawkeye. I'm glad you're here. I'm going to make this short because we have very little time. I'm doing a favor for Joe Stark, the usual security man at the park. He's down with the flu, and he asked if I'd stand in for him tonight. It's a good thing I did. Mrs. Lensky—you know, the lady who runs the ticket booth—says this guy robbed her about ten minutes ago. She was able to point him out to me, and I grabbed him and put the cuffs on him as soon as Mrs. Lensky made the positive ID."

"*This* guy," the youth sneered, "didn't do nothin'. That old bag picked me out because of my hair and clothes. But half the guys in this park are dressed like I am, or close to it. You don't have a case, Sergeant Dumb-well, and you know it. You didn't find no money on me, did you? And I've got two good witnesses who say I was on a ride when the money was taken. You hold me much longer and you and your Mickey Mouse police department are going to have a nice, fat lawsuit for false arrest on your hands."

As the youth spoke, Hawkeye pulled a somewhat damp sketch pad from his back pocket. His pencil darted about the page with deceiving ease, drawing, shading, then stopping for a moment for a detail to completely register. His artist's eyes flicked back and forth from the three young men to his sketch.

"You have witnesses, fine," Sarge said, "but whether or not they're good ones remains to be seen. Once again: you say you don't know either of these two young men?"

"I never seen either one of them before until just a few minutes ago."

"Then why," Sarge asked, "did they come forward as I was putting the cuffs on you?"

"Ask them. They're just good citizens, I guess," the captive answered sarcastically. "Aren't you cops always cryin' for people to get involved? Well, that's what these guys are doin'— gettin' involved so an innocent person isn't hassled."

The two toughs standing together smirked. "That's us," one said, "just plain good citizens."

Hawkeye nudged Amy. "Let's go talk to Mrs. Lensky," he said quickly. "This whole thing smells. I'd trust those guys about this much." He made a zero with his fingers and peered through it.

"Sarge," Amy said, "we're going to see Mrs. Lensky and poke around a bit. We'll be as quick as possible."

"OK, Amy," Sarge said, "but do your digging as fast as you can. Mrs. Lensky's resting at the First Aid Station, and someone's subbing for her at the ticket booth. Give this case your best shot. If we don't find a hole in this guy's story, I have to free him."

The youth in the handcuffs laughed. "Go get 'em, junior detectives," he said. "I seen that dumb story about you two in the paper. You're nothin' but little kids playin' cops 'n' robbers. So hurry up with your Sherlock Holmes bit. You and Dumbwell are wasting my val-u-a-ble time."

"Cool it, OK? If you showed more respect for the law," Hawkeye said, "you'd be an awful lot better off than you are now."

"Yeah? How, Dick Tracy?"

Hawkeye put his hands in front of him and then moved them slowly apart, until his arms were fully extended from his sides. "Let's see you do that," he said.

The handcuffed youth muttered something unpleasant.

Mrs. Lensky, a plump, usually cheerful lady of about 55, looked pale and frightened, and her hands trembled as she explained to Amy and Hawkeye exactly what had taken place.

"Twenty children and ten teachers from the Sunshine Camp for Special Children had just gotten their tickets," Mrs. Lensky said, her voice quivering. "Of course, we don't charge them. They had already moved on when the door of the booth crashed open and that—that—*boy* just pushed me aside and grabbed most of the money from the cash register. I was too frightened even to scream. Then he was gone.

"I yelled for Sarge when I got my breath back, and I pointed the boy out to him. He had the nerve to be standing at the hot dog stand, as calm as can be. Sarge grabbed him and was reading him his rights when those other two walked over and claimed that the thief was on a ride right in front of them when the robbery took place. Amy, Hawkeye, I *know* I'm not mistaken. Those witnesses—and of course the thief himself—are lying. But how can we prove it?"

"I'm not sure, Mrs. Lensky," Hawkeye answered, "but we'll do our best to find a way."

"Mrs. Lensky," Amy asked, "what happened next?"

Mrs. Lensky concentrated, bringing the events back to her mind. "Sarge took all three guys over to talk with Dick Clemens, who runs the ride. Dick couldn't help at all. He sees so many faces in the course of a summer, they're all a blur to him. Anyway, the thief said he was alone in one roller coaster car. The others said they were right

Hawkeye pointed to his sketch. "Here's the hole in the story!"

behind him, in the next car."

"Why was the guy alone?" Amy asked.

"He said he had met a girl and that she was going to go on the ride with him, but she got scared and decided not to go. He said he got angry and told her to get lost, then went on the ride alone."

"Did he mention this girl's name?" asked Hawkeye.

"He said her name is Sue, but he doesn't know her last name," Mrs. Lensky replied.

Hawkeye sighed. "There are probably fifty girls here tonight named Sue—and the one we'd be looking for probably doesn't exist, anyway. But thanks for your help, Mrs. Lensky."

The sleuths began to wander back toward the ticket booth. Hawkeye took his sketch pad from his pocket and studied his drawing for several moments, then smiled. He handed the pad to Amy.

"Look at this," he said, pointing to something. "We've found the hole in the story! Let's get back to Sarge and tell him he can make a formal arrest—and book the phony witnesses, as well!"

WHAT MADE HAWKEYE SO SURE THE THREE YOUTHS WERE LYING?

See page 91

The Secret of Sarge's Padded Cell

Sarge Treadwell leaned far back in his swivel chair. He nibbled nonstop from a large, half-empty bag of potato chips that rested on top of a pile of memos, Lakewood Hills Police Department reports, and FBI wanted posters on the desk in front of him.

"I'm not saying that you two aren't terrific sleuths, or that you don't investigate thoroughly and intelligently. I'm just saying that you may not be quite as effective as you think," Sarge said.

Hawkeye Collins grinned at Sarge. "When," asked Hawkeye, "was the last time we let you down?"

Amy Adams impatiently pushed her red hair

away from her forehead. "Better yet," she said, "when have we *ever* let you down? Sarge, we know you too well. You're setting us up for something. Right, Hawkeye?"

"Yeah," Hawkeye said. "Come on, Sarge. Out with it."

Sarge chewed and swallowed a large handful of potato chips before he spoke.

"A setup?" His eyes opened wide in mock innocence. "I don't know what you mean."

Hawkeye and Amy exchanged glances. Amy rolled her green eyes and shrugged, as if she had heard all this before.

Sarge leaned forward in his chair, rested his elbows on the desk, and made a steeple with his fingers.

"When I was in police training school almost thirty years ago, I learned something that has stayed with me ever since," Sarge said. "An FBI man came down from Washington to lecture our class. He stressed that as soon as you become overconfident, your effectiveness as an officer, a detective, or a sleuth drops like a stone down a deep well. You miss things—obvious things—at a crime scene. You stumble over clues without seeing them. And when that happens, you might just as well hang it up."

Hawkeye pulled his long legs under him and stood up. He began pacing about the office. "Are you saying," he asked, "that Amy and I have grown overconfident—and that we're working with you only to jack up our own reputations?"

"No, Hawkeye—and Amy. I know you kids like the challenge of your cases and the chance to help people. But I do want to ask you to keep both feet on the ground. To check you guys out, I want to propose a little bet."

"What's the bet?" Amy and Hawkeye asked together.

"Simply this: you've both seen the padded cell downstairs. It's used to confine prisoners who are physically dangerous to themselves or to others. There are four separate slide-bolt locks on the outside of the door. The hinges are concealed in the body of the door. There's no furniture in the cell—nothing at all. The walls, floor, and ceiling are padded with five inches of extrafirm foam rubber.

"The illumination inside the cell comes from four fluorescent lights, which are set into the ceiling. Of course, the fluorescents are protected by plates of bulletproof glass. There is a one-foot-square bulletproof glass window set in one wall, behind which is the observation room."

Sarge glanced at both kids, who were listening intently. "Prisoners in the padded cell are watched twenty-four hours a day. When the door to the cell is locked, the light in the observation room goes on automatically. The officer on duty in the observation room controls the light within the cell. The door is constructed of three-inch solid steel. The walls, ceiling, and floor are made of the same steel, under the padding. Air is circulated through a chrome-plated hardened steel grate in the wall above the door."

"Come on, Sarge," Amy said impatiently, "what's the bet? We've seen the padded cell—we know what it is."

"OK," Sarge said, "the bet: the three of us go into the cell. One of my people closes us in. You two get ten minutes to get us out." He paused. "Escape will not only be possible—it'll be ridiculously easy. I'll sit on the floor in the center of the cell for the ten minutes, and if you don't manage it, *I'll* get us out, using my hat as my only tool. I give you my word that I won't call or signal anyone. I'll simply use my hat—and my head—to get us out in thirty seconds. Agreed? And by the way, the loser buys us all hot fudge sundaes."

Hawkeye and Amy locked glances. For a long moment, there was silence. Then they both nodded slightly.

"Can we check your hat?" Amy asked.

"Sure," Sarge said, tossing his standard, visored police hat to her, "look it over all you want."

"And we have your word that there's no prearranged time for someone to let us out of the cell?" Hawkeye asked.

"Absolutely."

Hawkeye looked at Amy. She raised her eyebrows. "Sarge," Hawkeye said, "you've got yourself a bet."

Sergeant Treadwell beamed. "Good." He pressed a button on his telephone intercom. "Officer Ellis," he said, "would you please step into my office for a moment?"

In a few seconds, the door swung open. Officer Ellis, fresh from the Police Academy, had drawn a month of desk duty to familiarize herself with records and procedures before being assigned to a beat or a squad car.

"Yes, Sergeant?" she asked.

Sarge stood behind his desk. "I'd like you to close Amy, Hawkeye, and me into the padded cell. I expect that we'll be out in exactly ten minutes and thirty seconds. You are *not* to let us out, or allow anyone else to let us out, before that. Understood?"

Officer Ellis' face showed no emotion whatsoever.

"Understood, sir," she said.

"OK," Sarge said, "let's go downstairs."

Moments later, Officer Ellis hauled a heavy cell door open. Sarge followed Hawkeye and Amy into the padded room and, with some difficulty, sat in the middle of the floor, his hat in front of him. He was humming—slightly off-key—'Don't Fence Me In.' "

Officer Ellis grunted slightly as she put her

71

weight behind the door, pushing it closed. Sarge punched a button on his digital watch, then looked up expectantly.

Amy paced the cell, looking everywhere, missing nothing. She pushed and prodded at the padding in various places along the floor and as high as she could reach toward the ceiling along the walls. Hawkeye stood next to Sarge, concentrating on the chrome-plated air circulation grate.

"Two minutes gone," Sarge said.

Hawkeye crouched, then jumped as high as he could and smacked his palm against the grate. "Solid as a rock," he mumbled. "No way out through there, anyway." He began pushing at the corners of the room, hoping to discover some type of sliding mechanism. He found nothing but padding.

"Five minutes gone," Sarge said.

"The hat," Amy said suddenly to Hawkeye, "the hat. What can Sarge possibly do with that hat?"

"I don't know," said Hawkeye grimly. "If I did, we'd be out of here, instead of stumbling over one another like a couple of rats in a maze."

Amy walked over to a wall. "Can you come over here and boost me up? Maybe there's some sort of trapdoor up here! Hurry!"

"Eight minutes away," Sarge said. He began humming once again.

Hawkeye and Amy faced one another,

"Quick, do a drawing of this cell. We're missing something!"

frustration obvious in their eyes and on their faces.

"Hawkeye," Amy said hurriedly, "let's go for the one thing we haven't tried that's helped us so many times in the past—your sketch pad. Quick, as fast as you can, do a drawing of this cell. We *must* be missing something."

Hawkeye didn't take the time to answer. His pencil seemed to fly across the page, adding a line here, shading a perspective point there. "Finished!" he said. He dropped the sketch pad to the floor, and he and Amy knelt together, studying the page.

"You have forty-five seconds," Sarge said.

"Nuts!" said Amy. "We'll never—WAIT! Look, Hawkeye—we're out!"

WHAT GAVE AMY THE ANSWER TO SARGE'S SECRET?

See page 93

SOLUTIONS

The Case of the Missing Guests

The tracks gave the kidnapper's identity away. The main suspects were the unfriendly bike-hikers and little Curt Bingham. Hawkeye's sketch clearly showed that the tire tracks couldn't have been made by a pair of bikes. The tracks were simply too close together and too precisely parallel. But the tracks would match up with the wheels of Curt's wagon.

"Also, there was only one set of stranger's footprints, and they were small—several sizes smaller than Lucy's," Amy explained. All evidence indicated Curt had paid an unannounced visit to the tea party.

Sarah and Lucy ran to Curt's house. The animals and dolls were sitting in a neat line behind his garage. Curt had very much wanted to be invited to play with the girls, but neither Lucy nor Sarah had noticed him. Angry, he had hauled away all the "guests" in his wagon.

continued

77

Lucy and Sarah did invite Curt, and he
brought something to the tea party at least as
important as guests—warm chocolate chip
cookies, fresh from the oven.

The Case of the Fisherman's Favorite

The scrap of paper Hawkeye picked up was a receipt for fishing equipment. There is only one fishing equipment shop in Lakewood Hills: The Bait Shop, on Broadway Drive. Hawkeye and Amy pedaled there immediately after school. Hank Lewis, owner of The Bait Shop, remembered and described Macho perfectly.

"Mr. Lewis recalled, "I wondered at the time what a young boy with so little knowledge of fishing was doing with such an obviously fine fly rod." He sold Macho the fishing flies, line, license, and reel that were noted on the receipt.

Macho confessed to the theft and returned the fly rod when Sarge confronted him. Macho's parents grounded him for a full month—including weekends—except for the time he had to spend after school each day cleaning up at police headquarters.

81

The Case of the Toilet Paper Decorator

Hawkeye's artwork clearly showed a tall, fresh candle in the candle holder next to the easy chair. If Bad News had, as he said, been reading by the light of that candle for almost two hours, the candle would have been a short stub.

Under Sarge's questioning, Bad News confessed. "It just bugged me that Bronson could get me kicked out of school, so I got him. I should've realized that the T.P. wouldn't help, but I didn't—until Hawkeye and Amy caught up with me."

Bad News Thomas was very busy for several days with long ladders and trash bags.

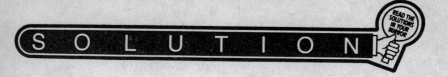

The Mystery of the Furry Lifesaver

There were two major pieces of evidence against Cash. First, his reaction to Stanley showed that it would be unlikely that he'd rescue a child. Second, Hawkeye's sketch showed that Nosey wore a leather collar, while Cash wore a chain-link collar.

"Since Steve Ruffino distinctly remembers a leather collar on the dog, Cash couldn't have rescued Stanley," Amy pointed out. In the end, Mrs. Terhune's reward check went to the National Blindness Research Foundation. Amy and Hawkeye happily accepted Mrs. Terhune's offer of giant ice cream cones—and Nosey got one, too. Margaret, however, claimed she was allergic to ice cream, so she and Cash didn't join in the celebration.

The Case of the Suspicious Soybeans

Although the table in Starshine's kitchenette was almost covered by fruits, vegetables, and other vegetarian foods, a wrapper from a package of hot dogs was visible in the wastebasket. With Hawkeye's sketch in hand, the two sleuths made a quick call to Sergeant Treadwell, who stopped Starshine in his colorful van at the edge of town. In his pocket was a check from Mrs. von Buttermore for $100,000.

"Man, you gotta be kidding! You're arresting me for eating hot dogs?" Starshine whined as Sarge read him his rights.

"No sir!" Sarge replied. "For selling soybean baloney."

Starshine ended up shining behind bars, and Mrs. von Buttermore promised to be far more careful in the future when approached by strangers with plans to save the world.

The Case of the Kidnapped Brain

Amy saw through Newton's strange message by reading only the first letter of each word, which yielded the message, "OLD MILL OLD MILL OLD MILL—" before Newton was stopped.

"It just seemed like such a dumb message from a brain," she explained, "I knew he was saying more than it seemed."

The police went to the old mill near Mrs. von Buttermore's mansion and forced the kidnappers to give up Newton without any violence. The gang members were convicted of kidnapping and sentenced to prison.

Since Mr. Pestle's cover was blown, he could no longer function as an undercover agent. He could, however, function very well as chief of detectives and special investigator for the Lakewood Hills Police Department. And his work gave him far more time with his wife and his very special son, Newton.

The Case of the Amusement Park Punks

Since the young men claimed to have been on the Over-the-Falls ride run by Mr. Clemens, all three should have been soaking wet, just as Hawkeye and Amy were. But Hawkeye's drawing showed three dry, dusty youths. It was impossible that they'd been on the ride, as they swore.

"If they'd been smart, they could've picked a ride where you don't get drenched," Sarge said, "and then our work would've been harder. But it goes to show you that crime appeals to some pretty dim bulbs."

In court several weeks later, Mrs. Lensky's testimony and the evidence developed by Amy and Hawkeye put the three youths in a reform school.

The Secret of Sarge's Padded Cell

Thanks to Hawkeye's sketch, Amy suddenly saw that the light in the observation room wasn't on—and realized that the door to the padded cell wasn't even locked!

Sarge had made it quite clear that the locking—not the simple closing—of the door would activate the light in the observation room. All Amy and Hawkeye needed to do was to push open the door and walk out—which they did with less than 30 seconds to spare.

"Like the old joke goes, I threw my hat in to make it hard," Sarge chuckled. "I knew it would draw your attention away from the fact that you could push the door open anytime."

Over hot fudge sundaes (at Sarge's expense), the two sleuths admitted that they nearly missed the obvious clue. Hawkeye summed up the situation well.

"Sarge," he said, "you lost your bet, but you proved your point. Amy's and my feet will stay firmly on the ground—where they belong!"

Dear Friend:

Would you like to become a member of the Can You Solve the Mystery?™ Reading Panel? It's easy to do. After you've read this book, find a piece of paper. Then answer the questions you see below on your piece of paper (be sure to number the answers). Please don't write in the book. Mail your answer sheet to:

> Meadowbrook Books
> Dept. CYSI-L
> 18318 Minnetonka Blvd.
> Deephaven, MN 55391

Thanks a lot for your replies—they really help us!

1. How old are you?
2. What is your first and last name?
3. What is your address?
4. What grade are you in this year?
5. Are you a boy or a girl?
6. Where did you get this book? (Read all answers first. Then choose the one that you like best and write the letter on your paper.)

6A. Gift
6B. Bookstore
6C. Other store
6D. School library

6E. Public library
6F. Borrowed from a friend
6G. Other (What?)

7. If you chose the book yourself, why did you choose it? (Be sure you read all the answers listed first. Then choose the one that you like best and write the letter on your paper.)

7A. I like to read mysteries.
7B. The cover looked interesting.
7C. The title sounded good.
7D. I like to solve mysteries.
7E. A librarian suggested it.
7F. A teacher suggested it.
7G. A friend liked it.
7H. The picture clues looked interesting.
7I. Hawkeye and Amy looked interesting.
7J. Other (What?)

8. How did you like the book? (Write your letter choice on your paper.)

    8A. Liked a lot   8B. Liked   8C. Not sure
        8D. Disliked   8E. Disliked a lot

9. How did you like the picture clues? (Write your letter choice on your paper.)

    9A. Liked a lot   9B. Liked   9C. Not sure
        9D. Disliked   9E. Disliked a lot

10. What story did you like best? Why?

11. What story did you like least? Why?

12. Would you like to read more stories about Hawkeye and Amy?

13. Would you like to read more stories about Hawkeye alone?

14. Would you like to read more stories about Amy alone?

15. Which would you prefer? (Be sure to read all the answers first. Then choose the one you like best and write the letter on your paper.)

    15A. One long story with lots of picture clues.
    15B. One long story with only one picture clue at the end.
    15C. One long story with no picture clues at all.
    15D. A CAN YOU SOLVE THE MYSTERY?™ video game
    15E. A CAN YOU SOLVE THE MYSTERY?™ comic strip.
    15F. A CAN YOU SOLVE THE MYSTERY?™ comic book.

16. Who was your favorite person in the book? Why?

17. How hard were the mysteries to solve? (Write your letter choice on your paper.)

    17A. Too easy   17B. A little easy   17C. Just right
        17D. A little hard   17E. Too hard

18. How hard was the book to read and understand? (Write your letter choice on your paper.)

    18A. Too easy   18B. A little easy   18C. Just right
            18D. A little hard   18E. Too hard

19. Have you read any other CAN YOU SOLVE THE MYSTERY?™ books? How many? What were the titles of the books?

20. What other books do you like to read? (You can write in books that aren't mysteries, too.)

21. Would you buy another volume of this mystery series?

22. Do you have any suggestions or comments about the book? What are they?

23. What is the volume number on this book? (Look on the front cover.)

24. Do you have a computer at home?

HAVE YOU SOLVED ALL OF THESE EXCITING CASES?

Volume #1

THE SECRET OF THE LONG-LOST COUSIN

Only $2.75 ppd.
ISBN 0-915658-81-X

A stranger arrives at Hawkeye's house from Alaska, claiming he's a cousin of Hawkeye's mother. But something bothers Hawkeye. So in the middle of the night, he creeps to the living room to study an old family photo. His sharp eyes pick up important clues... plus nine other mysteries!

HOW DOES HAWKEYE DECIDE WHETHER THE STRANGER IS A REAL COUSIN OR A PHONY?

Volume #2

THE CASE OF THE CHOCOLATE SNATCHER

Only $2.75 ppd.
ISBN 0-915658-85-2

A drugstore clerk reports that a masked thief has just stolen a small fortune in fancy chocolates. The getaway car leads Hawkeye, Amy, and Sergeant Treadwell to three suspects. Each of them has a perfect alibi, but Hawkeye makes a lightning-fast sketch and cracks the case... plus eight other mysteries!

HOW DID HAWKEYE KNOW WHICH SUSPECT WAS LYING?

Volume #3

THE CASE OF THE VIDEO GAME SMUGGLERS

Only $2.75 ppd.
ISBN 0-915658-88-7

Hawkeye, Amy and Sergeant Treadwell must catch the crooks who stole the video game their computer club just invented. At the airport scanner gate, Hawkeye sketches suspects who could be smuggling the disk. With seconds to spare, he and Amy pick out the thieves... plus nine other mysteries!

WHOM DOES HAWKEYE SPOT AS THE SMUGGLER, AND WHERE IS THE COMPUTER DISK HIDDEN?

Volume #4

THE CASE OF THE MYSTERIOUS DOGNAPPER

Only $2.75 ppd.
ISBN 0-915658-95-X

While Hawkeye and Amy are visiting Mrs. von Buttermore at her mansion, her Great Dane, Priceless, is stolen. Several people could be the dognapper, but Hawkeye and Amy take one look at the ransom note that arrives and immediately figure out who's guilty... plus nine other mysteries!

HOW DO HAWKEYE AND AMY KNOW WHO TOOK PRICELESS?

Collect all of Hawkeye's and Amy's cases—and solve 'em yourself!

Volume #5

THE CASE OF THE CLEVER COMPUTER CROOKS

Only $2.75 ppd.
ISBN 0-915658-11-9

Hawkeye and Amy must find out how someone stole hundreds of computers from a warehouse. The video camera in the warehouse was working the whole time, but the film from the camera shows the strangest thing—one minute there are hundreds of computers in the room and the next minute the room is empty. Hawkeye does a sketch of the warehouse and realizes how the crooks did it . . . plus eight other mysteries!

HOW DID THE CROOKS STEAL THE COMPUTERS?

Volume #6

THE CASE OF THE FAMOUS CHOCOLATE CHIP COOKIES

Only $2.75 ppd.
ISBN 0-915658-15-1

Grandma Johnson's cookie recipe is gone. Whoever stole it left a clue in the Cookie Works. Sergeant Treadwell needs the help of Amy and Hawkeye to crack this case. They find the thief with just a few clues. Can you? . . . plus eight other mysteries!

HOW DOES HAWKEYE SPOT THE RECIPE ROBBER FROM CLUES IN GRANDMA JOHNSON'S OFFICE?

Volume #7

THE MYSTERY OF THE "STAR SHIP" MOVIE

Only $2.75 ppd.
ISBN 0-915658-20-8

Amy and Hawkeye are visiting the set of their favorite movie, "Star Ship." Suddenly a man runs past them with a stolen copy of the film and the mystery begins. The thief is hiding somewhere on a set filled with robots and space ships. Amy uses Hawkeye's drawing to figure out who stole the film. Can you? . . . plus eight other mysteries!

HOW DOES AMY FIND THE THIEF HIDING AMONG THE ROBOT REPAIRMEN?

Volume #8

THE SECRET OF THE SOFTWARE SPY

Only $2.75 ppd.
ISBN 0-915658-25-9

Sergeant Treadwell knows that the spy who stole some computer software is going to eat at a fancy French restaurant. Amy and Hawkeye need to find the spy among the diners in a crowded restaurant. Hawkeye locates the prime suspect with only a few clues to go on . . . plus eight other mysteries!

HOW DOES HAWKEYE SINGLE OUT THE SOFTWARE SPY IN A CROWDED RESTAURANT

Collect all of Hawkeye's and Amy's cases—and solve 'em yourself!

FREE STUFF FOR KIDS

The latest edition has even more fun playthings than ever before! Over 250 of the best free and up-to-a-dollar things kids can get by mail:

Only $3.75 ppd.

- a sample of Mount St. Helen's ash
- a tiny blue spruce tree
- the Louisville-Slugger-Bat key chain
- Wizard of Oz stationery
- a strawberry plant
- a compass and booklet on orienteering
- and much more

Our Pledge: the suppliers have promised in writing to honor single copy requests. We monitor the suppliers and keep this book up-to-date and accurate.

ORDER FORM

Name _____

Address _____

City _____ State _____ Zip _____

Please charge my _____ Visa _____ Mastercharge Account

Acct. # _____ Exp. Date _____

Signature _____

Check or money order payable to Meadowbrook Press.

Quant.	Title	Cost Per Book	Amount
	#1 The Secret of the Long-Lost Cousin	$2.75	
	#2 The Case of the Chocolate Snatcher	$2.75	
	#3 The Case of the Video Game Smugglers	$2.75	
	#4 The Case of the Mysterious Dognappers	$2.75	
	#5 The Case of the Famous Chocolate Chip Cookies	$2.75	
	#6 The Mystery of the Star Ship Movie	$2.75	
	#7 The Secret of the Software Spy	$2.75	
	#8 The Case of the Clever Computer Crooks	$2.75	
	#9 The Case of the Toilet Paper Decorator	$2.75	
	#10 The Secret of the Loon Lake Monster	$2.75	
	Free Stuff for Kids	$3.75	
	TOTAL		

We do not ship C.O.D. Postage and handling is included in all prices. Your group or organization may qualify for group quantity discounts: please write for further information to Direct Mail Dept., Meadowbrook Press, 18318 Minnetonka Blvd., Deephaven, MN 55391.

Meadowbrook

18318 Minnetonka Boulevard • Deephaven, MN 55391 • (612) 473-5400